From the Beginning to the End

From the Beginning to the End

Henry Lewi

Chapeltown Books

British Library Cataloguing in Publication Data

A Record of this Publication is available from the British Library

ISBN 978-1-915762-15-3

This edition published 2024 by Chapeltown Books
Manchester, England

Contents

Introduction

Begin with the Big Bang and end with a distant trumpet call; understand how to send a cheese sandwich into the future, have the origin of the universe explained and find out how to achieve immortality; and finally add in a splash of espionage. Enjoy the mix.

In the Beginning

The Celestial Offices were in uproar; clerks, angels, and demons were running hither and thither, carrying sheaves of paper, instructions, and bulky files. The Celestial Board had decided on a Creation Program and the countdown to the Big Bang had started.

The black matter engineers rigged up the lighting sources; unfortunately some were highly unstable and quite a few exploded, sending an awful lot of debris out into the void.

"OK, OK," said the senior celestial engineer, "let them cool for a while but at least we've now got light that we can work by."

The scattered debris started to shine out there in the void.

"Well," said the celestial engineers "they were part of our office lighting sources – let them be; I'm sure they won't have an effect on our Creation Program – will they?"

In the celestial offices the lights began to flicker off, then on, and off and on again, with a monotonous regularity.

"Not doing any harm is it?" said the Senior Celestial Engineer. "It's quite pretty really, so if we can't fix it let's leave it – we can call it a 'Day/Night Program' – how about that?"

The Celestial Board weren't that happy, but agreed to monitor the situation.

"Let's address all that debris flying around in the void, so what are we going to do about all those rocks and fire globes banging into each other. Some of them are exploding, others are just hanging around," said the Chairman of the Celestial Board.

"Leave them be," said the Celestial and Black Matter Engineers. "We'll sort it, don't worry."

"We'll just throw some Dark Energy into the void; that'll calm it down."

So here they were three days into the program and the Big Bang hadn't even started. They had flickering lights and debris, and now the Black Matter Engineers were pumping Dark Energy and a splash of Dark Matter into the void.

The Celestial Board met for an emergency meeting. "Not going too well is it?" said the Chairman, as the various board members nodded their agreement.

"So when do we fire up the Big Bang?" asked the Chairman.

"Not just yet," said the Senior Celestial Engineer. "Let things cool down and in a day or so we'll send out a couple of observers to review the situation, report back and we'll see if we can get back on track."

The committee met again the following day; well the lights had flickered on/off and on again, and the Celestial Observers now reported back.

"It's all chaos out there," they reported.

"All this dark energy and matter has allowed the debris to expand outwards into the void. Some of the matter is cooling down, and they're forming into what looks like solar masses, and rocky planets that are now spinning on their own axes. You can all see this on the 'Giant-Omniversal-Display'." They indicated the current view of the universe on the massive screen behind the Celestial Chairman.

"Right," said the Chairman, "do we pull the plug on the Big Bang and start over?"

"Not just yet," said the Senior Celestial Engineer. "We could throw some normal matter into the mix and see what happens."

"Ok do that," said the Chairman, "but I'm setting up a Genesis subcommittee to monitor all this; you can report directly to them."

"Righto," replied the engineer, "I'll be sending out the observers again. They'll report back to me and the Genesis committee."

They were now into day five of their somewhat skewed Creation Programme. The Celestial Observers now reported to the Genesis Committee that on some of the spinning rocks various forms of Organic life were beginning to appear. The Genesis Committee escalated this up to the Celestial Board who now declared a Celestial Emergency.

The infinity-sized room was packed with Celestial Board Members, the Genesis Committee, Celestial Engineers and Observers plus the Host of Angels and the Legions of Demons.

"Right," said the Chairman, "where are we with this?"

"It looks like we have a runaway Autonomous Creation Programme," replied the Senior Celestial Engineer. "As you can see on the 'Giant-Omniversal-Display'."

"That's disappointing, how do we stop it?" said the Chairman as he turned to face the Giant-Omniversal-Display.

The G.O.D. suddenly displayed across its screen, "LET THERE BE LIGHT," and counted down from ten, and at zero, there was silence and the Big Bang happened.

The Sleeping King

It was the night before the battle. Grouped around their campfires, the men were confident, laughing, chatting and drinking ale. The archers checked their longbows, their bowstrings, their arrows, and sharpened their daggers and small axes. The foot soldiers sharpened their swords, pikes and daggers, and the cavalrymen fed their horses, and likewise checked their weapons.

Confidence was felt throughout the King's army encamped on the plain; to the left side was a dense impassable wood, and to the right side a swiftly flowing river. They knew that the enemy who were camped just a mile away would have to come directly at them in a frontal assault. They were absolutely sure that they would win, just as they had done countless times before, and probably would continue to do so. This time, thought the King's Commander, this time, maybe, just maybe, we can settle this war once and for all.

The war that had raged between the successive monarchs of both countries had been waged for over a century, and had resulted in numerous victories for the English Kings; many Peace Treaties had been made, and many had been broken. Men had died, trade had been disrupted and now was the time, to win this battle, ensure victory and finally put an end this long, long war.

Four English kings had led their men in war, with only one seeking a long lasting peace, and now this last king, this "Sleeping King" slept in his bed, in his Grand Palace in Windsor, safe in England, whilst his men fought and fell on the fields of France.

Before he had begun his long sleep, the King had screamed at his commanders, that he wished his war to be fought just like those of his father and grandfather, and those before them; to fight just as they had always fought their wars, with men, longbows and horses, nothing else would do. It was his legacy he said, "To Be Remembered That He Was As Good As They Had Been."

It was just before dawn when the King's army assembled in their massed ranks ready to receive the onslaught. Thousands of archers were massed on either side of the men at arms stationed in the middle of the army: foot soldiers in front, mounted knights behind, but all would be protected by the archers who would pour down volley after volley in a veritable rainstorm of arrows onto the advancing enemy. It had always worked, the King had said so, and the King had ordered it; so that was the way it was going to be.

As the King slept safely in his bed, his army waited in silence for the enemy to attack.

The sound of Trumpets and the pounding of drums from the enemy shattered the dawn peace and they could now see the enemy army slowly advancing towards them; as usual leading at their front were the massed ranks of heavily armoured warhorses ridden by their armoured knights, readying to charge down onto this Sleeping King's army. The earth shook with the slow advance of the armoured warhorses and riders; as the Sleeping King's army remained silent and still they could now see the steam rising off the warhorses and feel the thunder of their slow advance through their feet. Still the Sleeping

King's men waited in silence, waited for the enemy charge, waited for their Commander's signal.

The enemy's trumpets and drums continued, their horses stopped their advance and waited, the warhorses shaking their heads, pawing the ground and then the drums stopped and the enemies horses parted and moved to the sides of their advancing army revealing what seemed like row upon row of cannon, which suddenly opened fire. The king's men saw the flames, the clouds, and then heard the sound of the many cannon firing. The shot, the ball and the rocks screamed into the massed ranks of Foot Soldiers, Archers and the King's Mounted Cavalry, leaving screaming men, mangled bodies and great gaps in their massed ranks.

Still the King slept on, whilst history was rewritten, and warfare was changed forever.

The cannon continued to fire, row-by-row, cannon by cannon until the Sleeping King's army were completely broken, and those that could, fled the battlefield.

The enemy moved on and cleared their land of the hated English whist the "Sleeping King" didn't stir.

When he finally woke, the King found that all his lands in France, that he and his father and grandfather had fought over, were now lost. The King screamed at his Commanders and assembled Lords, blaming them all for the loss of his lands. The silent court watched as the King shrieked at them, and cried tears of anger and regret, and they silently watched as the King finally went mad.

A Day in the Life of a Silver Penny

The silver penny first changed hands at the farmers' market as part payment for a pig. The pig seller took his handful of coins to the nearest village alehouse and bought a jug of beer.

Later that day the recruiting team of a mounted sergeant, two of his men and a drummer arrived at the village inn, and set themselves up outside alongside their drum, promising free beer and a silver penny to every man recruited into the Kings army, to fight the French in Spain.

The recruiting sergeant sent one of his men into the inn to purchase the beer for the new recruits, and received the silver penny as part of his change.

They planted their regimental flag and beat their drum, with the Sergeant crying out, "Roll up. Roll up. Join His Majesty's Army. Receive a silver penny. Drink as much ale as you want. Roll up, roll up and join the King's Army."

One new recruit, Simple Jim, a farmhand, stepped up and received his bounty of the silver penny and beer and swore his allegiance to the crown.

"That's it lad, make your mark," said the sergeant. "You're now a King's man; we'll give you a fine new uniform with a smart red coat, white breeches and a hat. We'll give you a home and feed you and you will repay the King by fighting the French far, far away in Spain. Well done lad, drink up."

So Simple Jim made his mark, drank his ale and clutched his new shiny silver penny.

A couple of hours later as his head cleared and he decided he didn't much like the idea of fighting the French in some far off land, he made a bolt for freedom, swiftly followed by the recruiting sergeant who took him down with his sabre.

The 1779 silver penny that had been tightly clutched in the hand of Simple Jim, the King's newest recruit, rolled out of his lifeless fingers into a nearby ditch, only to be found by a detectorist some 250 years later.

A Problem with a Home Delivery

The place – Mount Olympus Home of the Gods

Dramatis Personae

Zeus
His wife Hera
Their Daughter Athena
Their Twins Apollo & Artemis
Ares God of War

Act I, Scene I

Zeus addresses the assembled Gods

ZEUS: Bugger all that "Thus Spake Zarathustra" rubbish; this is your All-Father Zeus Speaking. Now hear this – I, Zeus can't get a "Home Delivery" slot, we're running dangerously low on wine, honey and ambrosia and we've got to find a way of restocking. Mankind has lost respect for us Old Gods and won't provide any offerings of wine and ambrosia, and they're leaving absolutely nothing at the foot of Mount Olympus, so we desperately need a home delivery. Look, I've tried all the Major stores including that one called Iceland used by Odin and the Asgardians.

Apparently, there's no option for a "Major God and Deity Delivery" only for NHS staff and carers, and even Apollo, our God of Medicine can't access that option, as he's not employed by the NHS. Maybe Athena our so called Goddess of Wisdom has some idea of how to handle this?

ATHENA: Well Dad, I've been doing some research, and it seems that in the interests of diversity and equality, one group of Gods can't be singled out for preferential treatment. I was chatting to Thor, and he tells me that they are treated much better in Norway outside the EU. In Brussels we're not looked on kindly, as we have far more male Gods than female, so our EU Major Deity Grant is being slashed. I also blame the state of the Greek economy as well as the EU. The Greeks don't have two Euros to rub together and are now imposing additional taxes on any wine and ambrosia they give us. Is there any other particular reason why we can't get a home delivery slot; I thought it was open to everyone Men and Gods alike, so any ideas? Well anyway, here's one, I've heard – both Hermes and Cousin Nike have both set up their own online stores and delivery network; what about asking them? Or, how about we send a couple of the boys down to one of the supermarkets if we can't get a delivery or even organize a "click and collect" slot, if it's that desperate.

ZEUS: OK, thanks for that. Well folks, for a start Tesco, Sainsbury's and Waitrose won't deliver to our postcode; apparently OLY 8US is outside their delivery areas, and Harrods and Fortnum's won't risk their vans driving up the side of Mount Olympus. I know we haven't spoken to Hippolyta and her bunch of Amazons for over a thousand years, but I've heard that they've now set up a delivery business; maybe one of us could speak to them. Hera how would you feel about asking them to help us out?"

HERA: Right, fine, I'll give it a go, but you know things aren't great between us and the Amazons, ever since that bastard son of yours, Hercules, ran amok amongst them, got what, a dozen of those Amazon girls pregnant, and they all gave birth on the same day; what did they call it? Oh yes, the "Twelve Labours of Hercules". Anyway, we've desperately got to do some shopping now – you know I like to put honey on my Bran Flakes – us gods have to keep regular, and on top of that, look what's happened to my hair; I've run out of hair products and had to borrow some shampoo from Medusa, and now I've got bloody snakes on my head. So everyone, this is your mother speaking; you two, the twins, Apollo, and you Artemis get yourselves down to Tesco, as I hear they've got a two for one offer on honey and ambrosia. So what's the problem with that Artemis?

ARTEMIS: Mum! Do I have to? I've got a date with that Norwegian dish Balder the Beautiful this afternoon. Can't Ares go with Apollo. I mean he's got no major wars that he needs to be at, so he's got nothing to do, nor has that idiot bother of mine."

HERA: Fine, fine, go, go on your so-called date. Ares and Apollo can go and get the honey, ambrosia, wine and hair products and meantime I'll speak to the Amazons about getting a future regular home delivery.

A Crossword Clue

It was the 1st June 1944; the watery sunlight tried to pierce the smoke stained windows of the office in Praed Street London. The city was grey, the people were grey, and those buildings that remained intact were grey.

Despite the damage, London was packed with soldiers from many parts of the world: US troops, Czech and Polish soldiers, men of the Free French Army, plus the officers and men of the British Army.

The war was now taking a turn in the Allies' favour, with an invasion of Europe imminent. To the East the Soviet forces were relentlessly advancing and in the South of Europe the Allied Forces were slowly advancing up the leg of Italy. It was now clear that the invasion of Europe by the Allies was imminent.

In the offices of *The Committee of Awareness, Knowledge and Enlightenment*, Antoine Le Glaçage sat with his feet up on his desk blowing smoke rings towards the ceiling. He had been specifically and directly recruited from the SOE – Churchill's "Baker Street Irregulars" to provide some special services, as had his friend and colleague the Oxford educated Count Andrey Kozcinski, recently of Section II of the Polish Intelligence Bureau, who was seated slumped in the office's solitary armchair doing *The Times'* crossword.

In the ultra-secret and rarefied world of Allied Intelligence these Committee rooms, were known as "THE CAKE", and housed that section of Military Intelligence responsible for "housekeeping"; in simple terms the assassination and elimination of foreign agents active on British soil, and those individuals likely to endanger the security of the United Kingdom.

"Five down, *'wound my heart with a monotonous languor'*," read out Count Andrey. "Eight letters," he added.

"Isn't that a line from *Chanson d'Automme* by Verlaine?" replied Le Glaçage, who like the Count had read Classics at Oxford before the war. "Eight letters you say? Could it be the poet's name itself?"

"No," replied Count Andrey, "doesn't fit; one across definitely doesn't have a V."

"Ok so what's one across?" asked Le Glaçage.

"Right, one across *is 'too late for the party, the rat-catchers newest toy'* and that definitely doesn't have a V. OK, OK, maybe in the run up to the invasion I'm being a bit paranoid, but just follow my chain of thought," said Count Andrey.

"The Rat Catcher at the battle of Jutland was Admiral Beatty who commanded the Battle Cruiser Squadron. His newest ship HMS Renown was not quite ready, so he arrived after the battle and so 'his newest toy was too late for the party'. If Renown is the answer, then five down could be Normandy and it fits."

"Look," continued Count Andrey, "we know that the poem from Verlaine is the signal we're using to let the French Resistance know the invasion is on; the BBC have already transmitted the first line: *'Les sanglots longs des violons d'automne'*, which translates as 'The long sobs of autumn violins' and tells them the invasion is imminent, and our next line, *'wound my heart with a monotonous languor'*, means it's happening in the next forty-eight hours or so."

"OK," said Le Glaçage, "before we take it to the boss; are there any more possible clues that are likely pointers to the invasion?"

Scanning the crossword clues Count Andrey replied, "Bloody hell. Look at these four. Now this can't be a coincidence, can it, knowing what we know about the imminent invasion. There's got to be a leak somewhere, and these others give more information, look." He pointed to the crossword.

"OK, here goes and I hope I'm wrong, but it's unlikely. Twelve down *'Here a Goddess walks'* (four letters) that could be Hera or Juno, but the latter is the codename of one of the landing beaches; and fifteen across *'Orion sheathed it as Mars went downstairs'*, five letters, that's from *Charmides* by Oscar Wilde, and must be Sword, and yes it fits; it's yet another one of the landing beaches. Then there's twenty-one down: the clue is *'Young's territory achieving statehood'*, four letters. It can only mean Utah. That's one of the American beaches isn't it? And finally, here's one that really bothers me, twenty-eight across which uses the 'a' from Utah and the clue is *'A potent message that he's not in the game'*, six letters. I think that's Patton; he's head of FUSAG, the supposedly 'ghost' non-existent US First Army Group based in Kent and allegedly aiming for a landing in Calais. These clues are all devised by a compiler called Dolos."

"So summarizing," said Le Glaçage, "what we have here is a Times Crossword containing five clues to the upcoming invasion, all devised by a compiler called Dolos."

"So the question is: is he sending a message to German Military Intelligence, or is this just a coincidence? Right, let's go see the 'Chief'."

The "Chief" was a certain Colonel A.E.F. Farquarson, a World War 1 Veteran who had spent the early part of current war training the Stay Behinds, those extremely secret members of the Home Guard, trained in the dark arts of warfare, ready to commit assassinations, disrupt troop movements and perform random acts of terror in the event of a German Invasion. As the threat had long since passed Colonel A.E. F. Farquarson had been recruited to set up and run "THE CAKE".

The two entered the Chief's office and seated themselves; his desk was stacked with manila files mostly stamped with "Top Secret" in red.

"Gentlemen, we've an epidemic of possible enemy spies and we'll now have to work through them. So what have you got for me?"

Le Glaçage and Count Andrey slowly and carefully laid out their concerns and findings, illustrating their answers on the unfinished crossword.

"So," said Le Glaçage, "is this fact or fiction, treachery or coincidence?

"And who is Dolos?" asked Count Andrey. "We know he's the Greek God of Deception but who is he really? Well anyway in terms of the crossword compilation?"

"Right," said the Chief. "Let's do it logically. I'll phone Military and Domestic Intelligence to find out if they know anything. One of you contact the Times and get the real name of this so-called Dolos and find out who he is, where he lives and what he does. I think you two are going to pay him a visit, don't you? Let's meet back here in an hour and we can formulate our next steps, if any.

They reconvened in the Chief's office an hour later, and Le Glaçage read out the notes he'd taken regarding the crossword Compiler.

"He's a seventy-five year old retired teacher from Felsted School, currently living in a village called Dunmow, near the Essex town of Chelmsford. No obvious political affiliations, and as far as we can ascertain has never been a member of any pre-war pro-Hitler group. Supposedly he now lives alone and leads a quiet life, compiling crosswords, and gardening, and still does some tutoring for some of the boys at the school hoping to get into Oxford or Cambridge."

"Well," said the Chief, "both Military and Domestic Intelligence were surprised at your findings; they had absolutely no idea about this. They've both asked us at CAKE to plug the gaps. You two now have a free hand, so I suggest you pay this retired teacher a visit, today I think, don't you?"

The two returned to the offices of "CAKE" the following evening and reported to the Chief.

Sitting comfortably in his office both sipping from the glasses of Scotch that the Chief had poured for them, they gave him a full account of their trip to the outer reaches of Essex.

"It's probably a coincidence, just that, but we may never be sure. Sadly we can't bring him in for an interrogation as the poor man suffered a fatal heart attack not long after we left," said Le Glaçage.

"It seems that his sister's son– apparently she had emigrated to the United States at the turn of the century and married into an old New England family – her son as well as his nephew, is a Staff Colonel on Eisenhower's Invasion Planning Committee. He'd visited the old boy a week or so ago; they both drank too much whisky and then this nephew told him far too much about the plans for the upcoming invasion."

Le Glaçage took a sip of his Scotch. "So anyway, this Dolos as we'll call him, was tickled pink by all the names used in the planning, and thought they'd make excellent clues and answers for the crossword. Nothing more, nothing less, most likely an innocent coincidence; we don't believe there's anything sinister about it all; guess we'll never know, what with him now being deceased."

"Any links to us?" asked the Chief.

"Oh no," replied Le Glaçage. "The cottage is pretty isolated and we weren't seen anyway. So what about the loose-tongued Staff Colonel?"

"Leave that to me," said the Chief. "I'll speak to the Yanks in their Counter Intelligence Corps, wouldn't do for one of us to get involved in dealing with the demise of an American Officer."

Pausing for a moment, the Chief continued, "I suppose its case closed, just a coincidence of sorts. Good spot if I may say so, I just hope that German Intelligence don't have a penchant for doing The Times Crossword."

Space Command

When I was a young boy living in London, I used to read a weekly comic called *ZOR!* An amazing comic full of science fact, fiction and space stories; and best of all were the weekly adventures of Captain Rob, a space going explorer visiting far off planets, meeting aliens, and having all sorts of adventures in distant space, assisted by his trusty companion Alfie. (At nine years old I didn't think there was anything wrong with two men travelling around space for many months) The important thing was that Captain Rob could always communicate with Space Command back on Earth using his gold "Ultra-Communicator". Then one day *ZOR!* announced:

```
Get your own "Ultra-Communicator"
An exact copy of Captain Rob's
Communicator.
Use it to speak to your friends!
Use it to speak to Aliens.
Use it to speak to Captain Rob.
Collect 5 packet tops from "Grain
Crispies" plus a 10/- Postal Order and
the Ultra Communicator will be yours!
```

Well, 10/- or 10 shillings, (well, to you younger readers, that's the equivalent of 50p), was not quite a king's ransom but to a 9-year-old boy in

1959 it was still a lot of money. So, I ate Grain Crispies twice a day, saved up my pocket money, and the daily four penny bus fare by walking the one mile to school and back, and I took back bottles for their three penny deposit. And finally, finally, sent of the packet tops and 10/- postal order and waited and waited.

Then it arrived, I'd expected a brightly coloured box with pictures of Captain Rob and Alfie, but that wasn't the case; it arrived packed in a boring brown cardboard container – very, very, disappointing. Inside a message written in a spidery hand stated – Speak to us!

Holding my breath I unpacked it, and moved the big switch from OFF to ON: nothing, there was nowhere to put batteries in it, and repeatedly moving the switch did absolutely nothing. What a disappointment. Worst of all, it wasn't gold as in the comic but a dull grey. I put it up in my room and went off to play football with my friends in the local park. None of them had sent off for Captain's Rob's Communicator, despite all being fans of ZOR!

Late one night some weeks later, there was a hiss and a crackle and suddenly a voice stated, "Calling Space Command, calling Space Command. Can you hear? This is Captain Rob speaking. Hello Space Command. Over."

The Ultra-Communicator was now pulsing, and not only had it turned gold just like in the comics, but the ON/OFF switch had now turned a deep red.

I stared at it with amazement; I had never really given up hope that it would eventually work. I never expected that it would happen so quickly, and at night, but when you're a kid you accept things as they happen.

With trembling hands I picked up the Ultra-Communicator and moved the red ON/OFF switch to ON and whispered into it, "Hello this is Earth calling Captain Rob. Receiving. Over."

The voice answered back, "Is this Space Command?"

"No," I replied and gave Captain Rob my name and full address, adding, "I don't know Space Command. I'm here in London, England, and can I take a message?" I could get my Dad to speak to someone in Space Command in the morning.

"This is Captain Rob. We have an emergency and need urgent help from Space Command; it is vital you get this message to them. We are trapped on the rocky moon Zoton of the fourth planet of the New Magellan System in the constellation Aries. The Alien forces of the Evil Gila Empire are pursuing us, and two of our four rocket engines have been damaged. We need urgent advice on how to repair them and lift off from the moon Zoton, over."

This couldn't be right. I'd just read the latest adventure of Captain Rob which was just that, "his ship pursued by those monsters of the Evil Gila Empire had crashed on the fourth planet's moon Zoton in the New Magellan System in the constellation Aries". It was just that, and the adventure was titled "**Captain Rob escapes from the Empire of the Evil Gila Monsters**".

I had devoured every word, and had studied the illustrations carefully, and there in the centre of the comic was a four page illustrated pull out, showing just how Captain Rob and Alfie repaired their engines allowing them to escape from the moon and evade the clutches of the Empire of the Evil Gila Monsters.

I found the comic and turned to the centre pages, picked up the glowing now gold Ultra-Communicator and moved the red ON/OFF switch to ON and whispered into it, "Calling Captain Rob. Calling Captain Rob. Over."

"This is Captain Rob. Receiving. Over,"

"I have the plans on how to fix your engines. I can read them to you. Over," I replied.

And so I carefully and slowly read out the plans as described in the comic, picture by picture and word for word, and made sure Captain Rob heard and understood everything that had been printed in the comic about repairing the engines.

Captain Rob finally replied, "Bravo. Just the ticket; I'm firing up the engines."

A few minutes later the Ultra-Communicator beeped and Captain Rob's voice clearly and loudly came through. "By Jove," he said, "that worked like a dream; the engines are firing and we're taking off from the moon." And with that the Ultra-Communicator went silent, turned grey and the red ON/OFF switch stopped glowing red.

The Ultra-Communicator never worked again, and I never ever heard from Captain Rob again; was it just a dream? Well it could have been, but in the very next issue of *ZOR!* Which arrived the following week, Captain Rob's next adventure was highlighted by my name appearing as the Senior Space Command Engineer and gave me the rank of Colonel in the Space Command.

It was never a dream. It was all there in the comic, how I had helped Captain Rob and Alfie escape from the rocky moon Zoton in the New Magellan System in the constellation Aries, and escape from the Empire of the Evil Gila Monsters.

No, the Ultra-Communicator never worked again, and I never ever heard from Captain Rob. But it was OK, it was never a dream, as there was my name, right there in ZOR! There for all to see.

You Gotta Love a Pug

I mean you gotta love a pug; they're an adorable breed, fiercely loyal, easy to look after, and they don't require long walks; what's not to love about that. On top of that they're very pretty with their curly tail, perfect doggy stance and with their traditional fawn colour, black nose and ears, they stand out amongst the crowd. When they look at you with their dark brown almost black liquid eyes it'll melt even the coldest of hearts. What did I say? 'You gotta love a pug.'

Let me introduce you to my pug called Cosette or "Cossie". Yes she's named after one of the characters in *Les Mis*, bought by my daughter for my sixtieth birthday.

"At least you'll get out of the house once a day,' she said, "instead of sitting in front of your laptop all day long."

Well, at the time I was struggling with my second novel; the first was doing quite well, and there was some pressure from the publishers to finish the second.

So I did get out of the house, as we walked around the village, across the parks and along the riverbank in our Norfolk Village.

The quiet peaceful village was dog central; it seemed that every other person had some sort of canine pet. The shops and cafés all welcomed dogs, so there were no issues with having a quiet coffee, buying the daily groceries, and you could really go where you wanted. Cossie always behaved impeccably, never barked at other dogs or their owners. The other dogs would come up to her, either lie down alongside her, lower their heads or simply stand alongside, no matter the size or breed of the dog. There was never a barking competition, as other dogs seemed to have with each other; I really didn't think much of it at the time.

Well Pugs are somewhat of an exotic breed, loved by the Chinese Emperors, and worshipped as gods during the time of the Song Dynasty; and over the last few hundred years adored by the European Royalty. Queen Victoria apparently loved her Pugs and so did other members of her family, which included her grandson King George V. A touch of royalty perhaps, but who knows.

Anyway, the tranquillity of our village was shattered one day by the arrival of one of those so-called Biker Gangs, who rode down the quiet streets on their very noisy bikes, ran amok in the local shops, and threatened and terrorized many of the good village folk. They demanded money and valuables, stole bankcards and jewellery, and caused general mayhem, anxiety and worry.

Our solitary village policeman could do little to help, and quickly called for support and reinforcements from Norwich, but it would take some time for them to arrive in force.

I was out walking Cossie when I was confronted by half a dozen of these leather jacketed individuals, who demanded my watch, a Rolex if you ask, my wallet and anything else of value; I mean they were only objects so I was willing to give them up, but what was worse they kicked Cossie, grabbed her lead and threatened to hang her from one of the nearby trees. I tried to stop them but one of them hit me in the jaw, and I'm ashamed to say I collapsed like a sack of potatoes. As they dragged Cossie towards the tree there was a roar of thunder and a flash of lightning and where Cossie had had been appeared what looked like a female Chinese warrior. Yes absolutely, I kid you not.

Dressed in black armour over a dark red dress with a dark red cloak she carried one of those long Samurai swords with a second strapped to her back. Her long black hair was tied back into a ponytail and she looked mean, and ready for business. Within seconds my assailants were laid out, I won't describe the wounds but they didn't look pleasant, and this what, Dog-Warrior or God-Warrior? Strode off into the main village and from what I could hear was effectively dealing with my assailant's comrades, and quickly returned to where I was laid out on the ground.

Lifting my head she kissed me on my forehead, and I stupidly asked her, "Who are you?"

"I'm Cossie," she replied. "Others may know me as Panhu the so-called Dragon-Dog, your protector," and with that she disappeared and there was my Cossie sitting next to me.

Of course the police arrived and tried to get some sense from the villagers and me; the Biker Gang were strewn around various points of the village, many badly injured, loss of limbs, etcetera, etcetera, and the police had trouble making sense of it all. The description of an armour wearing Chinese Warrior

34

was assumed to be due to group hysteria, and the story of my dog becoming a sword wielding avenger was put down to the fact that I was an old man, who had been knocked out by the Biker Gang, and was just a confused rambling old fool.

The final police version was that the Biker Gang had been attacked by a "person or persons unknown" acting as vigilantes, and had subsequently disappeared.

Over the years Panhu has never returned, and I've often thought that after being knocked down I had dreamt the whole episode, but Cossie has truly earned my respect; I mean you gotta love a pug!

The Asteroid Murder Act

He had arrived safely at Lunar Moon Base Alpha after having fully served his sentence in the Asteroid Mining Belt.

The twenty-five year sentence for murder had been reduced to ten years as he had agreed to serve his time in the Penal Mining Colony on the Asteroid Vesta; mining for the many Rare Earth Metals, found on the cold, isolated Asteroid. The work was hard, dangerous and relentless; nevertheless, those who agreed to serve their time in the mining colonies could expect a significant reduction in their sentence, whatever the crime committed, as well as a substantial bonus on their return to Earth.

The murder of the man directly responsible for the ruination of his family, the death of his parents and brother was "'the crime", the sentence the payback, but at least in his own eyes he felt that justice would have been served.

When he landed at the Lunar Moon Base with a couple of others who had served their sentence, he was duly processed by the United Nations Off-World Penitentiary Service, or as it was always called, "The UNOPen". Forms were signed, new clothing provided and there was an exhaustive medical.

He was in good health despite the ten years in space; in spite of the hard labour and difficult conditions, the food had been plentiful and nutritious, the quarters comfortable. The mining of these metals was after all, necessary and crucial to the Earth's economy. With an annual fatality rate of nearly thirty per cent due to the treacherous conditions, the convicts had to be maintained in good health and good spirits.

For the convicts, there was nowhere for them to run, escape was impossible, and with the Lunar Base a three month journey away, where could the prisoners escape to anyway?

After all the checks, form-filling and medicals were completed, the now freed men had some time to wait for the next shuttle to take them back home to Earth.

A member of the UNOPen together with a senior member of the UN Justice Department now met him, and assigned him two bodyguards, in preparation for his return to Earth.

It was now that things became serious.

Seated around a table in one of the meeting rooms in the Lunar Base, the designated UN Justice Officer asked, "Have you selected your target?"

"I have," he replied.

Having fulfilled the requirements of the "Pre Crime Sentencing Act of 2215" and having fully served his sentence for murder, he was now able to go and commit his designated and registered crime under the full protection of the United Nations Charter.

The scales of justice would now be fully balanced.

Notes on Time Travel I

"Can you really travel back in time, without there being consequences?" asked the President.

"Yes, Madam President," replied the Scientist, "and today we will prove it. And there will be no consequences."

"Today, we will witness the first transportation of a living animal backward in time using captured tachyons. As the particles bombard the subject it will disappear and reappear in exactly 3.84 seconds."

As, anticipated, the subject disappeared and reappeared in exactly 3.84 seconds.

The US President stood up, and said, "Wonderful, wonderful: World Beating US Tachyon Technology!" He was still wearing his trademark red baseball cap and tie...

Notes on Time Travel II

The trouble with time travel is that it is full of dilemmas. You go back in time. Is it your past or an alternate reality past and the same thing when you travel forwards in time, whose future is it or when is it?

Those scientists working in the Transient Particle Unit where they'd originally identified the tachyons, together with high energy and sterile neutrinos spent a lot of time pondering this dilemma. These researchers had first noted that those particles both appeared and disappeared instantaneously, and their mathematical calculations and modelling inferred that the particles were able to travel both backward and forward in time. So, the theory was, that if you bombarded an object with these transient particles, depending on their velocity you could propel an object either backwards or forwards in time.

The Cheese Sandwich Test was the basis for time travel. In their first series of tests the scientists were able to send a cheese sandwich (mature Cheddar if you ask) backward in time, initially for ten seconds, then for longer periods of time and finally for twenty-four hours.

How did they know this? Well, they sent it back to their own lab where the scientists had already logged the arrival time of the sandwich, which they already knew, as it had already happened anyway.

Are you following this so far?

Now the important thing, dear readers, is that each sandwich was freshly made before being sent back in time, so it was whole when it left and whole when it arrived. So, the cheese sandwich as it bounced back in time followed a coherent timeline – it was made, sent back in time, and returned to its original timeline intact and as fresh as it was when sent.

Confidently the scientists turned their attention to the exciting prospect of the transportation of the cheese sandwich into the future.

They repeated their tests sending the cheese sandwich ten seconds, ten minutes, and ten hours into the future – smooth as silk. It was when they got more adventurous and started sending the cheese sandwich further and further into the future, that they then hit the dilemma.

A cheese sandwich was sent two weeks into the future, it departed smoothly and immediately returned to the point of origin with a large bite taken out of it.

The scientists examined, measured and X-rayed the bite, and repeated the experiment the following day, sending the original, now not so fresh but partially eaten cheese sandwich back into the future. The re-sent cheese sandwich reappeared at its point of origin but now as an intact freshly made cheese sandwich.

The team shut down their experiment, and waited for the two weeks to elapse until firstly, the whole cheese sandwich they'd sent into the future appeared, which it did – a perfect cheese sandwich with a bite taken out of it – the partially eaten sandwich appeared, shimmered, and disappeared back into the past, but they already knew that.

They waited on the following day when the partially eaten cheese sandwich they had sent into the future two weeks earlier now reappeared as a freshly made completely intact cheese sandwich and as before it shimmered, and disappeared back to its point of origin.

OK folks so answer me this: how can a cheese sandwich made fresh today and sent into the future as a whole sandwich return to its past with a bite taken out from it?

Even more of a puzzling dilemma was the question of how could a partially eaten cheese sandwich sent into its own future now reappear at its point of origin as an intact freshly made cheese sandwich?

The scientists could only conclude that somewhere in the timeline that they had created, the two or was it only one cheese sandwich had crossed timelines, or had they really?

What would have happened if they hadn't sent the second, or was it really the first cheese sandwich into the future a day later?

Was this a time paradox, where the one cheese sandwich that went back and forwards in time had re-crossed its own timelines, so there was only one cheese sandwich appearing at two moments in time simultaneously?

If that was the case, how could the one cheese sandwich appear at two differing moments in time?

Was there an extra cheese sandwich floating around in the universe of time waiting to be eaten, that had somehow been created by their experiments?

Was there a point in time when the one cheese sandwich momentarily became two sandwiches? Then as the sandwiches re-crossed their timelines the two became one.

The scientist couldn't answer that question, but one of them suggested that they should repeat the cheese sandwich experiment, but this time using two sandwiches sent simultaneously; one a classic cheese sandwich made with mature Cheddar, and the other a cheese and pickle sandwich, as the time travellers.

A Bit of a Chat and a Cough

(COUGH, COUGH). You know I've always been a thief; in fact I come from a long line of thieves – it's all I know. Yes, yes, yes, **(COUGH, COUGH)**. I've tried other jobs, but they've never worked out. My Pa, **(COUGH, COUGH)**, he used to say to me, "Take what you can from the world, you don't owe it anything," and he must have been right as Her Majesty was always very keen to entertain him; as he used to say I've always been at Her Majesty's Pleasure **(COUGH, COUGH)**.

Myself, I keep as fit as I can and every couple of years, I go into a detox program sponsored by Her Majesty's Government – the gyms are pretty good and you get three square meals a day with no alcohol and I always leave leaner and fitter than before I entered the program, **(COUGH, COUGH)**.

Like I said, I've had other jobs, the best being working as a car mechanic, when the customers always let me use their cars for a few days so I can get around – I mean every little bit helps – I always remove their number plates when I go out at night – I suppose it helps a bit.

As I said I've always done a bit of thieving and these lockdowns have helped a bit I mean there's nobody around especially the Old Bill, **(COUGH, COUGH)**. Sorry, I dunno, my cough seems to have got worse since this last job with the oldies, **(COUGH, COUGH)**. I'm sure it's not the rollies; you know I try to limit it to a couple of ounces a week, **(COUGH, COUGH)**.

I'm a strong believer in the old "Quick in, Quick out" – only pick up small items and jewellery, just enough to go into my shoulder bag, never more – the rule is "Don't get greedy", and you'll be OK, (**COUGH, COUGH**).

Like I said, quick in and out, and always go for houses the oldies live in; they don't have these alarm systems or cameras and go for the side gate and back door.

Rule number one – there are no rules; but never ever hurry – look as if you mean to be there, park around the corner (**COUGH, COUGH**), but remember there are no rules.

Take this last little job **– (COUGH, COUGH)**. Now I think of it, I didn't have a cough before that last (**COUGH**), job, 'scuse me, I'm just going to get some water – I dunno I'm a bit short of breath (**COUGH),** and my chest feels a bit tight, anyway as I was saying – this last job OK.

The house was all dark, no lights. It's one of those between the wars detached houses you know; they're all over London – not posh but middle class like. I knew that the elderly couple living there were alone, and it being two o'clock in the morning unlikely to be up. There was no obvious alarm, so I went by the side gate you know what – the oldies never lock them, (**COUGH),** and tried the back door to the kitchen, which was unlocked, pushed open the door, (**COUGH**). I mean I've done this so many, many times before, and as the local paper and that last judge said it's my Mogus Hoperandi, (**COUGH**).

You can always count on the judge to help educate you, and as he said to me, "Burglary is in your blood; it's all you know," (**COUGH**). But it's not like I rob multiple properties in the same street – "just the one", I like to think. I mean London's large enough to work every night without having to go back to the same street, (**COUGH, COUGH**).

Yeah, sure it's getting harder with all these alarm systems and cameras being fitted. But you know what, the older the occupant the less likely they've fitted an alarm, and there's usually a decent haul. I don't touch electronics – can't understand the bloody things, (**COUGH**), I go for the jewellery and cash; stuff that I can put into my shoulder bag, (**COUGH**). I mean they've got to be easy to carry, store and get rid of. (**COUGH, COUGH**).

Anyway the house was silent, and I spotted a small figurine on the hall table that neatly fitted in my bag. Anyway I climbed the stairs and pushed open the door to the first bedroom. There were no sounds I could hear, but I could see there were two people in the bed, but no movement, absolute silence.

You know what, I didn't have this cough then, so I didn't make any sounds and nor did they. So anyway I had this torch and shone my light onto the couple who were clearly asleep; WELL, I'm SURE they were, weren't they? There was no sounds, no movements, and I couldn't hear any sounds of breathing, (**COUGH, COUGH**).

Next to the old man in the bed had a there was a big gold Rolex. I can always spot one, and a signet ring on the table on his side of the bed, which I removed, and he didn't shift. So, I did the same with the other bedside table, removing another watch – a ladies Cartier I think, a diamond pendant and pearl necklace that were on her bedside table and removed a few other items of jewellery from around the bedroom, **(COUGH, COUGH)**.

Anyway, I didn't want to hang around, so I quickly left the house. *Quick in, quick out*, I thought, leaving.

You know I'm grateful to the Virus, as thankfully with lockdown due to – what do you call it a Pingdemic or what? – **(COUGH, COUGH)** there are very few people and cars about, certainly no Old Bill.

I don't feel so good at the moment, so I guess I'll have to cash in my haul when this lockdown is over, **(COUGH, COUGH)**.

Ten days later the Intensive Care Unit Nurse switched off his life support. "Pity," she said behind her protective mask and visor. "I thought we could save this one."

The Great Game

It was the summer of 1949 and in the greyness of post war London; an unseen war was being waged. The huge wave of refugees, ex-military, and freed enemy POWs hid amongst them spies and intelligence agents from the unseen enemy.

For days, ex-SOE operative Major Antoine Le Glaçage, and his colleague the Polish Count Andrey Kozcinski, lately of Section II of the Polish Intelligence Bureau, had been tracking the movements across London of a so-called German Citizen deemed a "Man of Interest" by the Intelligence Service.

The gentleman in question had been an operative of German Military Intelligence the so-called *Abwehr*, and a member of the Anti-Hitler faction, who had personally surrendered to the Allied forces in Paris in August 1944.

Having spent the best part of two years being debriefed, the ex-*Abwehr* military intelligence officer had been allowed to settle in London and was now supposedly living quietly in North West London.

Le Glaçage and Count Kozcinski were now observing the ex-*Abwehr* agent's movements as he travelled by both bus and tube across London, and around the outskirts of what was now being called Metroland, which now included London's outer suburbs of Wembley, Pinner, and Ruislip.

Once a week the ex-*Abwehr* agent would travel by bus from his home in Wembley to the Lyons Corner House at Marble Arch, have lunch and take the bus back home.

A few days earlier the pair had been summoned into the Chief's office and handed a black-tabbed Manila folder containing the details of the man they were shadowing.

Their Chief, a certain Colonel A.E. F. Farquarson led their department, formally known as "The Offices of The Committee of Awareness, Knowledge and Enlightenment" but now known as "The CAKE" in Whitehall circles. It was that section of Military Intelligence responsible for "housekeeping", in simple terms the elimination of foreign agents active on British soil and those individuals likely to endanger the security of the United Kingdom.

"The gentleman in question is one Erich von Staffel, who is your next target. He is an ex-*Abwehr* officer, who was a close friend of Admiral Canaris, the old boss of German Military Intelligence, a somewhat dysfunctional organization, not very effective, very anti-Hitler during the War, and the rumour was that they worked hand in glove with British Military Intelligence from 1936 onwards. In addition to that, this gentleman studied at Cambridge in the early 1930s before joining German Military Intelligence in '36, and so, is fluent in English, and somewhat familiar with English life. The orders from higher up are to firstly watch this man, establish who his contacts are, and then in your own inimitable style ensure that he is eradicated. We have been informed from those in the know, is that he is now most likely working for the Soviets and probably has been since before '39."

So here they were, travelling backwards and forwards by bus, tube and occasionally by car, watching and observing, as their target crisscrossed

North-West London. The only item of note was that Von Staffel always carried a copy of *The Times*, whose crossword he always attempted during his journeys to his selected destinations.

Once a week he travelled to Eastcote near to Pinner, in what was now becoming part of a post-war expanding London, where he had tea in the cafeteria in the grounds of Eastcote House, a place Le Glaçage noted was frequented by the staff who worked at the nearby newly renamed GCHQ Headquarters, that had taken over most of the duties carried out by the men and women of the Government Code and Cypher School, that had previously been located at Bletchley Park.

On other days he travelled to the Lyons Corner House at Marble Arch. He seemingly met no one and he spoke to no one; he merely read *The Times*, did the crossword, had a cup of tea sometimes he had a sandwich or a piece of cake and left, returning home by bus or tube, closely followed by both Le Glaçage and Count Kozcinski. A solitary existence thought Le Glaçage; this was the lonely life of a spy.

Le Glaçage and Count Kozcinski kept to the shadows, watched from a distance and seemingly remained unobserved, though on occasion they thought that they themselves were being followed, and that they were the watched, not the watchers.

"You know," said Count Andrey Kozcinski, "I think I've found the answer; at both places he goes to the Gentlemen's lavatories with his copy of the Times, and simply returns, but yesterday at Eastcote, he did just that, but on his return journey home he was doing the crossword and seemingly filling in squares that I had watched him solve on his journey out, but this was now on a fresh crossword. He's definitely swapping papers in the Gents' toilets and either leaving or dropping off messages via *The Times;* the crossword is just for show."

"So," said Glaçage, "you think he picks up something at Eastcote and drops something off at Marble Arch?"

"Just so," said Count Andrey. "And if everything stays the same, his next visit will be to the Corner House at Marble Arch. So we'll let him leave, we'll stay and watch and see if anyone pays a visit to the Gents and then wait and see if they come out with a copy of *The Times* newspaper. Do you still have your miniature Minox camera?" he asked Le Glaçage. "By the way, do you feel as if we're being watched?"

"I had that feeling a couple of days ago, but can't shake it. Yes I have the camera and we'll photograph all those men leaving the Gents; they won't all carry a copy of *The Times*. We'll then see if we can match them with anybody in the 'guest books' that we know that are attached to the US or Soviet Embassies. Then we'll try and repeat it at the other end, in Eastcote. Whatever it is, the leak must be coming from someone at GCHQ, and Von Staffel must be the courier between the two, friend or foe, enemy or not; let's get to the bottom of this as soon as we can."

They watched and waited, and two days later von Staffel caught his bus to Marble Arch and as was his usual practice, entered the Corner House where he proceeded to drink his tea, eat a sandwich and do the crossword.

As always he met no one, spoke to no one, and paid a quick visit to the gentlemen's lavatory, finished his tea and left, but this time Le Glaçage and Count Andrey stayed where they were.

Over the next two hours ten men entered and left the gentlemen's lavatory; Le Glaçage, using his miniaturized camera, photographed all those men as they entered and left.

Back at their offices at CAKE, they had the photographs developed, and were comparing them with photos of known men attached to both US and Soviet Embassies whose photos were inserted into what were known as "Guest Books" when Count Andrey let out a loud "Aha, got him."

"What we have here is a certain Sergei Pavel Ivanovich, currently a commercial attaché in the Soviet Embassy; he's the number two in their department. Previously he was an officer in the NKVD Border Guard; this must be von Staffel's Soviet contact."

"You sure?" asked Le Glaçage.

"Definitely," replied Count Andrey. "Here, see for yourself; this is certainly our visitor to the Lyons Corner House at Marble Arch." He passed over the Soviet Embassy Guest Book.

"Yup that's definitely him," replied le Glaçage. "Right, let's take it to the Chief."

The two entered the Chief's office and seated themselves; his desk as always was stacked with manila files mostly stamped with "Top Secret" in red, to which a number of differing tabs were attached. Black tabs meant terminate immediately, blue meant treat with the utmost caution and prepare to terminate, and finally yellow meant watch carefully and review the case in the next couple of months.

"Gentlemen," said the Chief, "as you know we've an epidemic of enemy agents and spies here on our shores, not always the obvious enemy. By that I mean the Soviets. We also have the Yanks, the French and various others watching us, and we have to tread very carefully. So what do you have for me regarding our dear friend Erich von Staffel?"

Le Glaçage and Count Andrey laid out their findings, observations, photos, and thoughts relating to their monitoring of the ex-*Abwehr* agent, and his visits to both Eastcote House and the Lyons Corner House at Marble Arch, together with the probable role of *The Times* and its crossword.

"We both think we've been watched at some point, but it's only a feeling," said Le Glaçage. "But no matter. Anyway our next step is to identify the person who may be the leak from GCHQ at the Eastcote end."

They watched von Staffel as he started to make his way to the Underground station; they knew that if he took the tube from Wembley Park, he would take the Metropolitan line directly to Eastcote station, and then make the five-minute walk to Eastcote House.

As the ex-*Abwehr* agent walked toward the tube station, a truck travelling at speed mounted the kerb and hit von Staffel, throwing him into the air, and rapidly drove away. It had all happened so very fast, Le Glaçage and Count Andrey had little time to react.

The two of them ran over, but with von Staffel lying in the road, his neck at an abnormal angle, it was clear that he was dead. As the crowd gathered and the police arrived, Le Glaçage and Count Andrey slipped away.

When they returned to the Offices of the Committee of Awareness, Knowledge and Enlightenment it was in silence; quietly they entered the Chief's office and sat down.

"I've heard," said the Chief, "of an unfortunate set of affairs."

"From what I understand from the Yanks, you were right; they were watching you two, and likewise the Soviets had also made both of you too. Neither of them are sure who you are, but realise you're both with a branch of British Intelligence, and the Soviets now realise that you had identified both their courier, and their Embassy man, who by the way has been sent back to Moscow, presumably to face a firing squad. Well, that's Stalin for you. Anyway they needed to protect their source so have removed the last remaining link; that's von Staffel. At the moment we don't know who their agent in GCHQ actually is, but we'll find him; don't worry about that."

The Chief continued, "It was always going to be tricky; that's why Rudyard Kipling called it the "Great Game". Sometimes we win, sometimes the other players win, but we try and move forward; we're all just pieces on the game board."

"So what I suggest," said the Chief, "is that you two keep your heads down, hide out for a month or so. May I suggest you both go to Wales? Here's a couple of files relating to certain Welsh businessmen with interesting connections they made during the last war; you can deal them," and passed over a couple of sets of files marked "Top Secret". "Deal with them and then return to London. Let all dust settle and let all the players get back into position. And maybe then we can sort out the leak at GCHQ. Just remember, it's been an unfortunate set of affairs, that's all, and it's all part of the Great Game."

"Good luck. See the both of you in a month."

Immortality – Is It Really forever?

There were five of them; they'd shared a house for the last two years whilst they completed their degrees at Cambridge. Maggie, Susie, and Harry had continued their studies, and all three were now enrolled in PhD programmes. Of the remaining two, Ben having recently graduated with a first class degree in Economics had decided to go into Politics and was attempting to get selected for the upcoming by-election in Newmarket, as a potential Conservative Candidate; and Ralph or Rafe as he preferred to be known, a "Cambridge Blue" was continuing his medical studies, but remained part of the Cambridge University Boat Club, hoping again to be a member of the eight man crew taking part in the annual Oxford and Cambridge Boat Race.

Susie and Ben were a couple, but their rowdy relationship veered from very much on, to intermittent splits; currently they were a pair, despite Ben's right wing political views.

The student house itself was atypically tidy, especially in the kitchen and living room; the fridge was full, drink bottles carefully stored away, and the empties always discarded in the appropriate bin; they never knew when an inquisitive parent might turn up!

Maggie and Susie, who were both pursuing their PhDs in Greek Art and Archaeology, were away that summer, both on a dig somewhere around the foothills of Mount Olympus in Greece. Harry was now attached to the Institute of Astronomy, working towards his PhD.

Summer had ended and the new academic term was dawning, when the two girls returned from their summer dig, tanned, fit and slimmer than before their departure. They excitedly told their tale of a newly discovered temple and sacred well dedicated to the little known and completely forgotten god Aion, the supposed ancient Greek god of eternity. They described how this god of Eternity may have been a later version of Kronos, who was the primordial god of time, but in this temple the interpretation was that of a male youth trapped within the circle of time and that image had appeared at the entrance to the temple and at various points around the central circular sacred temple well.

"And yes," they both said, "there was still water within the well, iridescent sparkling water, a deep blue aquamarine in colour, and yes it had been sent off to the labs in Athens to detect for bacteria, viruses and poisons; of course none were found," the two of them chorused, "and no, nobody had drunk it – of course not."

The archaeology team had also brought back numerous samples to Cambridge for further analysis and study, they said.

"Guess what," said Maggie. "We have our own sample here in our flask," which she waved at them.

"Anybody want to try it? It shimmers and sparkles but it's harmless. So do any of you want to try something that's over 3000 years old, bug free and won't do you any harm?"

Harry asked, "Any warnings in the temple or in the old texts you two have studied?"

"None that we can think of," replied Maggie.

"Well, except that one at the entrance to the temple," added Susie, "but it wasn't exactly a warning though, more advice, and translated as 'do not aspire to immortal life, but exhaust the limits of mortal life'. That's it, nothing else."

"Interesting," said Harry. "Well it's good to have you both back though; anyway, can't stay. I'm due at the Institute tonight. I'm one of the team on the overnight telescope array. See you all tomorrow morning. Have fun."

"OK," said Susie, "let's have a bit of fun and drink some of this 3000-year old water." She poured out the shimmering iridescent deep turquoise coloured fluid into four glasses. "We'll leave some behind for you Harry, to have when you get back."

When Harry got back early the following morning, as soon as he stepped into the house, screams, groans, the sound of crying, and shouts of "Oh my God what's happening?" greeted him.

"It must be Susie and Ben at it again," he thought; their history for the last two years was one of break up and make up, and this most definitely sounded like make up. He took a quick drink in the kitchen, and began to climb the stairs, but was greeted by shouts of "Don't come up. Stay where you are, but don't come up," and more screams.

"What's happening?" he yelled from the foot of the stairs.

He was answered by Rafe shouting, "Just stay where you are; we'll try and come down to you," and Susie crying out. "Has anybody got some proper sunglasses? Throw them into my room. Don't come in. Whatever you do, don't come in." In the background Maggie was sobbing and shouting "Help me, please help me."

"OK," said Rafe, "I've got my sunglasses I use for rowing; they're powerful top of the range UV400. Will they be good enough? I'll leave them outside your door; and hey, what's up with Ben? He's very, very quiet."

"OK, so what's going on?" yelled Harry again.

"Don't ask," said Susie, "and thanks for the glasses; and when I come down don't look at me. Ben rushed into my room, and when I looked at him he turned to stone, and what's more I now have snakes on my head; that fucking drink has turned me into what? A Gorgon you know, like that Medusa in the old stories, so whatever you do, don't look at me."

"Yeah," said Rafe, "that drink has turned me into some sort of half-goat or half-sheep. I mean you've got to see my legs, and I've now got hooves and a bloody tail. I'll never ever be able to row again. All I want to do now is drink wine, chase a nymph and play a flute. I say Harry old friend," he yelled out, "You haven't by any chance brought a nymph with you, have you? Will Ben be all right?" he added, without drawing breath.

"He's fucking stone; I've already told you that," said Susie.

"I know what you said, but will he be all right?" asked Rafe again.

"No, he's stone. Get it? He's solid, immovable and made of stone. Of course he won't be all right. He's a fucking statue."

"Right, right," said Rafe. "It'll wear off won't it?"

58

"How in God's name would I know?" screamed Susie. "This has never happened to me before."

"What's going on?" yelled Harry again. "I'm coming up."

"Don't," shouted Susie and Rafe together.

"What about Maggie? I can hear her crying. Should I see to her?" said Harry with one foot on the bottom of the stairs.

"OK, OK, said Susie. "Look I'll close my door, as will Rafe; you go up and see to Maggie. Yell out when you're in her room, and the two of us will go downstairs and meet you there. I'll try somehow to make sure the sunglasses work, and so hopefully I won't turn anybody else to stone."

Harry bounded up the stairs and quickly entered Maggie's room, yelled out "OK," and closed the door. He was confronted by a now grey-haired Maggie looking toward him sightlessly; both her eyes were missing, and there in the palm of her hand she was holding a solitary eye which turned towards him as he entered the bedroom.

Between sobs she said, "I woke up this morning, couldn't see out of my left eye and when I sneezed my right eye fell out. I can still see everything with it, but it's right here in the palm of my hand. If I didn't know better, I think I've become one of the Graeae; the supposed myth is that they are three sisters who share one eye between themselves, and can see into the future, but I'm not really sure if I'm one of them, or one of the Three Fates. It must have been that 3000-year old water we drank last night"

"Ok," said Harry. "This is all a bit odd. Are these changes permanent or temporary and any way to say the least, should I take you to the Eye Hospital where they might be able to help?"

"In a bit," replied Maggie, who seemed to have calmed down. "If it was that water we drank last night, hopefully the effects will wear off in a few hours. Let's go downstairs and see the others."

So Harry slowly led Maggie downstairs. She carefully held her eye out in front, as she followed him, and they met up with the other two in the kitchen.

Susie was now wearing Rafe's powerful UV400 sunglasses, the snakes hissing and writhing on her head.

"It's OK. I went out the front door just now. Mr Ahmed from next door was going to work. I looked directly at him and said, 'Hello.' I must say he looked at me very strangely, but with me wearing these sunglasses at least he didn't turn to stone, not like poor Ben. So what kind of hair products do you think I'll need for the snakes?" she said with a laugh.

Harry just stared at her, and then at Rafe, "Mate," he said, "you're going to need a hat to cover those small horns on your head."

"What?" said Rafe, feeling the top of his head. "Yeah I guess so. Can you nip out when the shops open, and get me a baseball cap, a flute and see if you can rustle up a couple of nymphs, failing that a goat or a sheep. Not being too fussy, am I?"

"You're also going to need some baggy jogging pants, and Rafe, put some underwear on, OK. It's not a good look trotting around with everything hanging out, and with those legs you really do look like a half goat; I mean you can't go out just wearing nothing but a pair of Y Fronts and a baseball cap," added Harry.

"Let's just sit down and take stock about what's happened, and try and solve this problem."

So they sat down around the large Kitchen table, Harry at the head, to his left Susie with her head full of hissing writhing snakes, wearing a pair of dark blue UV400 sunglasses, to his right Rafe, the half man now half goat ex-Cambridge University Blue, and at the other end of the table sat the grey-haired, eye-clutching Maggie, who carefully held her solitary eye in the palm of her hand as it now moved and watched everybody.

"Firstly, what do we do about Ben? He's due at his selection interview tomorrow. He can't go if he's turned to stone and where are we going to keep him? And what do we tell his parents? Oh, by the way, your son's ex-girlfriend turned your only son into a stone statue. They'll really, really believe that, won't they? I suppose, politically speaking, Ben as a statue has as much to offer as any other Conservative candidate, and likely more to offer than that last living breathing human Conservative MP, so no real loss there. I suppose his statue could still get selected to stand in the next by-election. Not sure anyone would notice."

"Right. Seriously, this all happened to you three overnight, after you drank that what, 3000-year old water from the Well – yes? Do you all think it's temporary or irreversible and what's going to happen now? I mean, Susie, you really can't go into college with snakes in your hair, and wearing sunglasses, can you? Maggie, we need to sort out this eye issue and fast; you can always dye your hair. Grey doesn't really suit you. And what about you Rafe? You can't go on your clinical attachments, never mind your rowing, with the legs and hooves of a goat, and playing a flute, and the least said about your tail and horns the better. By the way, what's' your first clinical attachment anyway?"

"General Practice, in one of those rural Cambridgeshire GP practices: plenty of wood-nymphs, goats and sheep out there," replied Rafe.

"Really Rafe. Get a grip will you? This is serious," answered Harry.

"Anyway I think this is temporary, and we'll all get back to normal in a few days at the very longest," proclaimed Susie.

"I don't think so," said Maggie. "Remember as one of the Graeae I can see into the future, and in that future we still are the same, plus we're now immortal." Shaking her head, she intoned in a deep voice, "We Have Drunk From The Timeless Well of Aion."

"Why didn't you say that shit before we drank the water?" said Susie. "Now I'm a Gorgon, Medusa to be exact; that idiot Rafe is likely to be that airhead god Pan, who has only three things on his mind: sex, wine, and playing the flute. And you're now a one-eyed mystical Seer."

"I didn't know," said Maggie. "It's the Graeae talking, not Maggie." The eye in her hand swivelled backwards and forwards between speakers.

"Fine, fine," said Harry. "So if you're all immortal, it's like forever, yeah? So what are the three of you going to do? I mean forever is a very, very long time, and I'm not sure that Cambridge or the UK is going to be able to deal with three immortals living in its midst. At some point, Susie, your glasses will slip off, or you'll forget them, and somebody else will turn to stone. Rafe, there just aren't enough wood-nymphs in the world to keep you interested forever, and what are you going to do, Maggie? You can't walk around always, holding your eye in your hand; at least let's get you fixed up at the Eye Hospital."

"Wait," said Maggie as she leaned forward, and then looked up, and magically she had both her eyes, repeating the movement, the solitary eye was now in the palm of her hand. Finally, again demonstrating the manoeuvre for a third time, the two-eyed Maggie now looked at Harry, and replied, "I don't think so, do you?"

"How did you know how to do that?" asked Harry.

"I don't know," Maggie, replied. "I just did, so there's no need to go to the hospital is there?"

So they drew up a shopping list: baseball hats for both the snake-haired Susie as well as Rafe, loose fit jogging bottoms and a flute for Rafe, three extra pairs of UV400 sunglasses for Susie, plus some simple lubricating eye drops for Maggie.

Harry went back upstairs to take a look at the statue that was Ben, a solid, immobile, and unmoveable figure; there was little he could do. What can you say when your best mate is turned to stone by his ex-girlfriend?

Shopping done, items delivered, Harry caught up with his sleep, leaving the three to now discuss their endless future, and how to cope with living in the modern world.

That evening Harry left for his second night at the Institute of Astronomy, and when he returned the following morning, the house was empty; all three had left; and the statue that had been Ben had disappeared. Harry knew that he'd never see them again.

Of course the police were called, and he spent many, many hours being interviewed and questioned, but Harry could shed no light on their disappearance. He had been at the Institute the night they had left and would the Police ever believe that Susie had become the "Gorgon" Medusa, and had turned her ex-boyfriend to stone? That another housemate had become a one-eyed immortal mystical seer, and the third had become the flute playing woodland god Pan? Not on your life.

To escape the publicity, Harry transferred to Caltech in Pasadena in the US, where he completed his PhD, eventually becoming a full Professor in the Department of Astronomy.

Harry never heard from the three of them again, though over the years he would occasionally hear or read news reports that clusters of stone statues would be discovered in isolated spots across Europe, and Harry knew that the "Gorgon" Medusa that had once been Susie was still thriving. There were now reports that the woodlands of Europe were teeming with wildlife, and he assumed that that was down to Rafe, or was he now the full-time Pan? As for Maggie, he had heard that a new oracle had sprung up in the foothills of Mount Olympus, worshipped and protected by the locals and the Greek Government; was that her?

One day he'd try and visit, but not just yet; after all, he had all of eternity right?

That mouthful of the 3000-year old water he had drunk that first morning had turned him into Zeus, Lord of the Sky, King of the Gods, complete with Thunderbolts.

They were all now immortal right? But was it really forever?

Bear It with Pride

Ever since he was a very young lad he'd watched his team play, and had dreamed the dream of being part of that close bond of men. He'd travel with the supporters to the home and away matches, always comforted by the men and supporters around him.

In his early and late teens he'd trained hard, followed the tight schedules of diet, exercise and team participation.

Then finally encouraged and supported by the others, he had the courage to get the required team tattoo, which he now wore with pride, and revealed, at every opportunity.

He was ready, his fitness was never in doubt, nor was his physique; he was finally selected to the exclusivity of the first team.

The day dawned and he made his way to the Home stadium; he'd been given the number 10 in his team, and they now stood in line ready for the kick off.

As the whistle blew, all fifteen members of the team removed their shirts and faced the crowd, the tattoos emblazoned on their chests. All those members of the "Team" bore the name of their beloved football club with pride; all the men were of a similar age, size and shape, none with a BMI below 40; and there he was, "The Number Ten", proudly bearing the massive tattooed U of United on his chest. There in the home stand the row of fifteen tattooed men spelt out the name of their beloved club, he was finally a part of his boyhood team, truly a dream come true.

I Wish This Wasn't True

The recent discovery of the previously lost fifth volume of Jean Froissart's works on medieval history has now uncovered the profound effect that the Alien presence and interference had upon medieval society.[1]

Let me quote from the translation of this newly discovered work:

> "Here written are the chronicles as recorded by Master Jehan Froissart, which speak of the recent wars between France, England, Scotland, Spain, and Brittany, the fifth volume of which I now refer to the presence of those non-earth beings and the names of the lords who were involved in these affairs.
>
> "In order that the honourable deeds accomplished by arms, which took place during the wars between France and England, might be properly documented and commended to lasting memory, so that men might follow such examples to inspire them to good, it is my wish to undertake to record this glorious history, which will be divided into firstly four parts, the fifth part, that being devoted to those not of this earth who have with divine intervention held sway among those royal courts of France, England, Scotland, and Spain.

---

[1] Chronicles of Frossart – The newly discovered Volume V; Bonnover College History Department, Bonnover university press, (2011). www.bonnoverhistory.com

"In the year of our Lord 1346, the English under the command of their most beloved King, Edward III of that name of the House Plantagenet, did visit upon the massed armies of France commanded by our Gracious Lord John the Good, son of our noble King Phillip the Fortunate, together with the men of Flanders and Bohemia, led by King John the Blind, a most terrible slaughter, with Our Beloved King Edward victorious in all aspects of the battle.

"The Scottish Kings had long made welcome those not from this realm, and many amongst them became advisors to those same Kings, amongst them the most noble Kings, Malcolm, Robert the First, known as The Bruce, and King David of Scotland.

"In England, Our Beloved King Edward also made them most welcome, promising them freedom and land for their help in his noble war against the King of France.

"These unearthly advisers brought with them the Ribauldequins and Culverins; these are most terrible weapons that shoot flame and ball at the enemy from a far distance. They also brought with them the Longbow so that the English could fire their arrows with power and strength into the noble French King's forces. Such weapons had never before been seen in all of Christendom and such was the slaughter imposed upon the

French by the English King, our Pope, the 'Holy Clement VI', ordered that such weapons be not used again, declaring that such use of the Longbow, Ribauldequin and Culverin were an anathema in the eyes of the Holy Church.

"The English victory at Cressy near to the town of Crécy-en-Ponthieu has changed the course of warfare forever. English men-at-arms were now able to pursue unopposed chevauchées across the Kingdom of France, and took the Port of Calais as their prize."

With regard to the Black Death Froissart wrote, and these are his exact words:

"The pestilence which had first broken out in the land occupied by many of those not from this world, notably in the Eastern Lands, was likely brought by those beings from their otherworldly homes, and spread through all the dominions it visited, with the scourge of sudden death in all of Christendom, destroying the greater part of the people.

"It began in England about the feast of St. Peter, in the year of our Lord 1348, and immediately advancing from place to place it attacked men without warning. Many of those who were attacked in the morning it carried out of human affairs before noon. And few whom it willed to die, did it permit to live no longer than three or four days."

This fifth volume of Froissart's Chronicles is the first written work to definitively record the presence and profound influence that non-Earth Aliens had upon Medieval Society.

The Watch

It was 4 am; he stumbled out of the bar where he'd been celebrating with his friends. Not for him the clubs and bars of Soho, for him it was the more refined upmarket area of Knightsbridge.

He'd left the bar alone, and was making his way home when a tall good-looking woman accosted him and asked, "Looking for fun and company, honey?"

Muttering, "No thanks," he found he was suddenly surrounded by one, two, he counted six hooded young men, who pushed him against a wall demanding his watch and anything else he had of value, with one pushing a large knife under his chin.

"OK, OK, there's no need for violence," he said as he undid the strap of his watch and was about to hand over his expensive timepiece.

"And your wallet, and your phone, you rich bastard," said another of the youths.

Then it was all over, in a manner of seconds; all six lay flat out on the ground, unconscious, dreaming of what, he didn't care, as he retrieved his belongings. Using his phone he called the police using a number he'd been given the day before; they seemed to arrive in a matter of minutes, all black clad and armed.

"We'll sort this out, Sir," said their obvious leader. "Best get yourself off home. Do you need a lift?"

"No I'm fine," he replied. "The walk will clear my head, thanks."

He watched as the six who had now recovered consciousness were bundled into a police transport. He checked the time on his watch.

Turning over his very expensive Patek Philippe he reread the inscription engraved on the back, which said – WELCOME HURRICANE – NEWEST MEMBER – UK SUPERHEROES plc. – 2024.

War Came

Then out of the spring and summer days the War came.
It came in the shape of grim helmeted men dressed in grey.
It came in the shape of iron monsters that rode over people, houses and our
    soldiers.
It came in the shape of shrieking war planes, dropping bombs and killing all
    around us.
We ran, we fell,
Some got up, many did not,
Still they came.
They killed; they advanced
They didn't stop until they met our Greatest General
He held their advance,
He grounded their planes
He froze their iron monsters.
Thank God for General Winter, our saviour.

Leaving the River

They'd left the river many days ago and sailed on into the open sea.
The prow faced west and the sail billowed.
For seven long days the ship sailed; it seemed going nowhere.
At night there were no stars, and they didn't see the sun rise or see it set.
One moment it was night, the next it was day.
Their armour and shields were stored in the centre of the ship
The oars of the longboat were stowed.
From somewhere the wind blew them on; where, they didn't know.
They had no hunger they had no thirst.
Still they sailed on,
The ship of dead Viking Warriors sailed onward to Valhalla.

The Attack

They faced each other across the field.
Fully trained.
Fully Fit.
Both sides wore their distinctive uniforms.
They were ready, oh so ready, and eager for the off.
The signal was given and the attack was on.
The young men charged forward.
It seemed so easy, as they broke through the enemy's defensive line.
There it was as the watching crowd screamed
"GOOAAAL!"

The End

It seemed like it took forever for him to finally wake up.

He heard the sound of a distant trumpet.

He knew he'd been asleep but for how long and where was he?

He tried to move his arms, legs and wings but it seemed as if they were encased in something.

Slowly, gradually, he could begin to move his arms and head, but his wings remained stuck, fixed and splayed out on either side.

As his vision cleared he looked around and he could see he was hanging, fixed by those wings to an arched roof somewhere deep underground.

Coloured lights flicked on and off, and far, and far below he could make out streams of people, watching him.

His memories returned but not in any particular order; the last one seemed to involve a massed battle with his brother Lucifer, and in the far off distance he could hear a trumpet being blown.

Was it a call to arms? It was all so confusing.

He tried to remember.

There had been an argument with the so-called Supreme Being, something about the creation of man. What was it? He couldn't remember.

From somewhere in his mind a memory about some bearded bloke called Daniel and his involvement with lions appeared, some writing on a wall; was it a message, graffiti or what?

Was that really, the cause of him being here, stuck like this?

Then the image of a flaming sword flashed through his mind; what was that about?

Anyway, where was he?

He strained his wings but they wouldn't come loose.

More memories came flooding back.

The battle.

The defeat.

Yes, now he remembered.

Lucifer had triumphed and now walked the Earth. Mankind had joined his brother's side and they now ruled the World.

He'd been asleep for far, far too long.

He struggled and strained his wings and at last they came free and he dropped to the floor.

He was here in the deep cave that the locals had named after him, located deep within the mountains at the far end of a continent.

He folded his wings and left the cave and reached the open air at the highest point of the Rock and looked out to the distant sea.

He again heard the sound of a distant trumpet; he now remembered his brother Gabriel's signal.

He knew the forces were assembling.

He spread his wings and he rose into the sky; he stretched out his hand and the flaming sword appeared, and the Archangel Michael flew toward the End of Days.

Like to Read More Work Like This?

Then sign up to our mailing list and download our free collection of short stories, *Magnetism*. Sign up now to receive this free e-book and also to find out about all of our new publications and offers.

Sign up here:
  http://eepurl.com/gbpdVz

Please Leave a Review

Reviews are so important to writers. Please take the time to review this book. A couple of lines is fine.

Reviews help the book to become more visible to buyers. Retailers will promote books with multiple reviews.

This in turn helps us to sell more books… And then we can afford to publish more books like this one.

Leaving a review is very easy.

Go to https://amzn.to/4hkOStF, scroll down the left-hand side of the Amazon page and click on the "Write a customer review" button.

Read More of Henry Lewi's Work in These Books

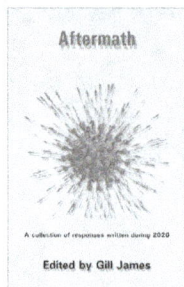

The 12th Crusade and *The New Hope* in
Aftermath
Published by Chapeltown Books (2021)

Order from Amazon:

Paperback: ISBN 978-1-910542-74-3
eBook: ISBN 978-1-910542-75-0

Martha and *Letter to Madelyn* in
Best of Café Lit 12
Published by Chapeltown Books (2023)

Order from Amazon:

Paperback: ISBN 978-1-915762-03-0
eBook: ISBN 978-1-915762-04-7

Other Publications by Chapeltown Books

Soaring
by Nicole Fitton

Small chunks of life, perfectly wrapped and waiting for you to open! Stories told in 70-1000 words.

Award-winning and short-listed pieces of prose sit alongside newer thoughtfully crafted short glimpses of human nature and 21st century life. You are invited to pause for a moment and reflect on the writer's suggestions. They are sure to uplift and inspire you.

"Beautiful, enchanting and so cleverly written!" *(Amazon)*

Order from Amazon:

ISBN: 978-1-910542-97-2 (paperback)
978-1-910542-98-9 (ebook)

Chapeltown Books

The City of Stories
by Lynn Clement

What goes on behind closed doors? Donna and Jim struggle with an unspeakable act. Millicent encounters something that will change her forever, and Marie dreams of being free from her harrowing life. Melvin's pelvic thrusts have his clients in a sweat, and Sister Francis, the bike-riding nun, has her secret revealed.

The City of Stories is a collection of short, easy-read stories and poems that range from dark tales with a twist, to funny flash fiction that will make you laugh out loud.

"An art gallery full of vivid word pictures." *(Amazon)*

Order from Amazon:

ISBN: 978-1-910542-81-1 (paperback)
978-1-910542-82-8 (ebook)

Chapeltown Books

Between the Lines
by Pam Line

The author gives us glimpses into a life full of interesting and wonderful stories. Chance encounters, happy events and tragedy mix into a melange of experiences. This anthology is an attempt to capture truth, possibly somewhat exaggerated, and shows our daily lives in a pared-down fashion, in snippets that appear important with a sheen of incredulity. Most of these tales are true, some even verbatim.

Between the Lines takes us on a roller-coaster life adventure.

"All human life described with a smile." *(Amazon)*

Order from Amazon:

ISBN: 978-1-910542-68-2 (paperback)
978-1-910542-69-9 (ebook)

Chapeltown Books